SPACEBUNZ

VOLUME 1

ART AND STORY BY
INOBY

ADULT READERS ONLY

This is a work of fiction.
All characters, events, and locations portrayed within are fictitious.

SpaceBunz: Volume 1

Published by Bewere Books
Flagstaff, Arizona
https://www.bewere.net

ISBN 978-1-62475-159-2

Printed in the United States, United Kingdom, or Australia
First printing February 2022

Cover and interior art by INoby

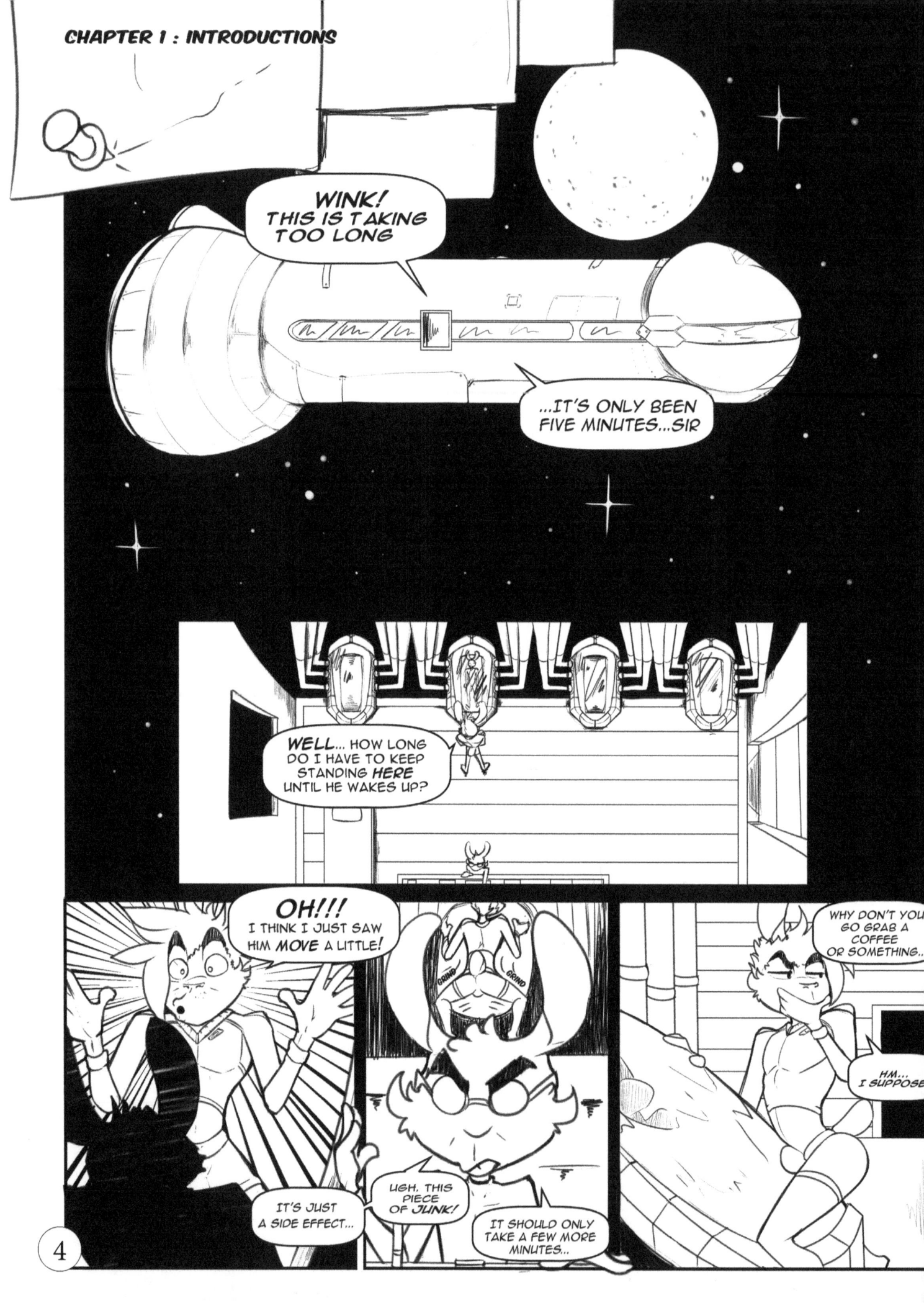

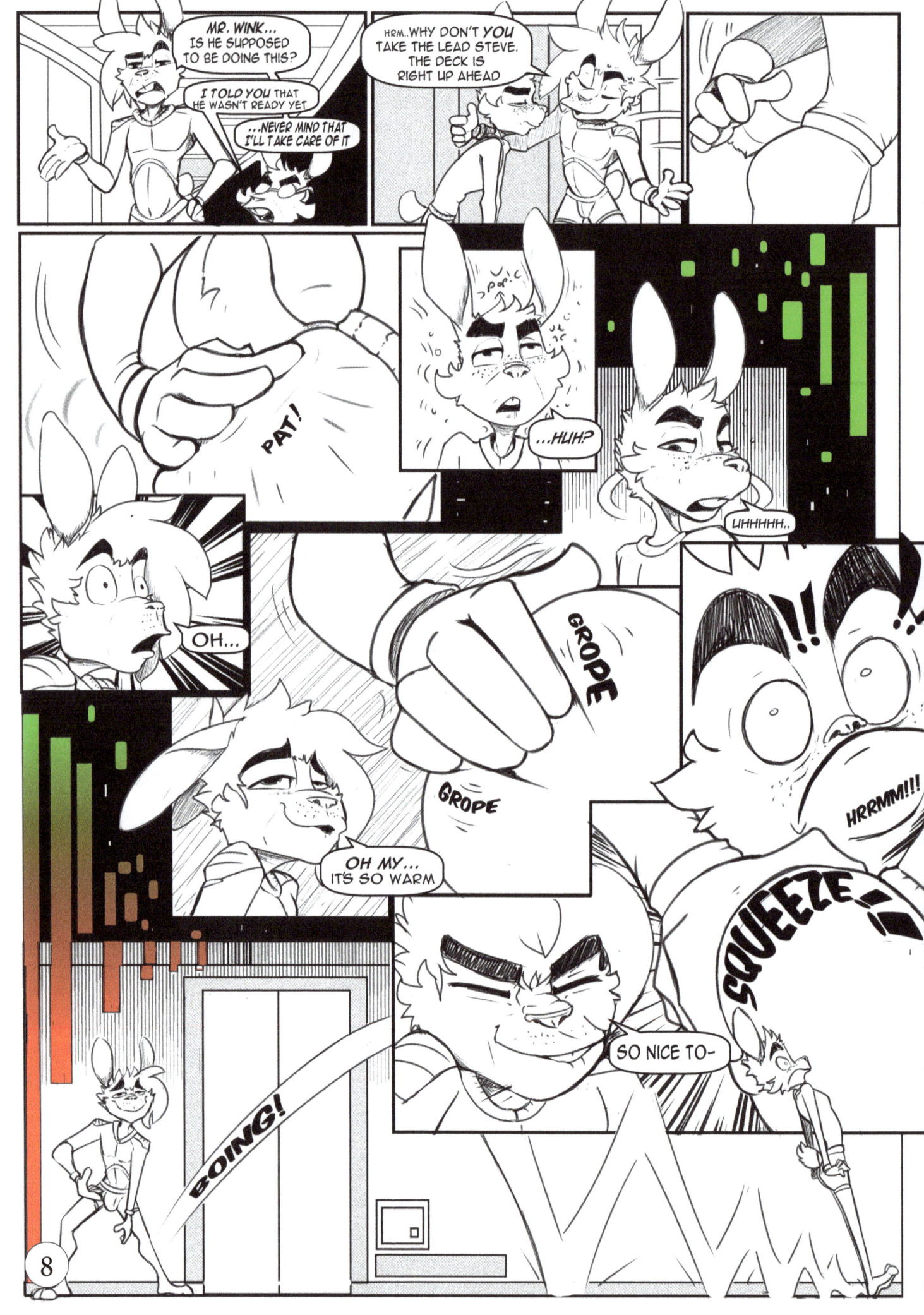

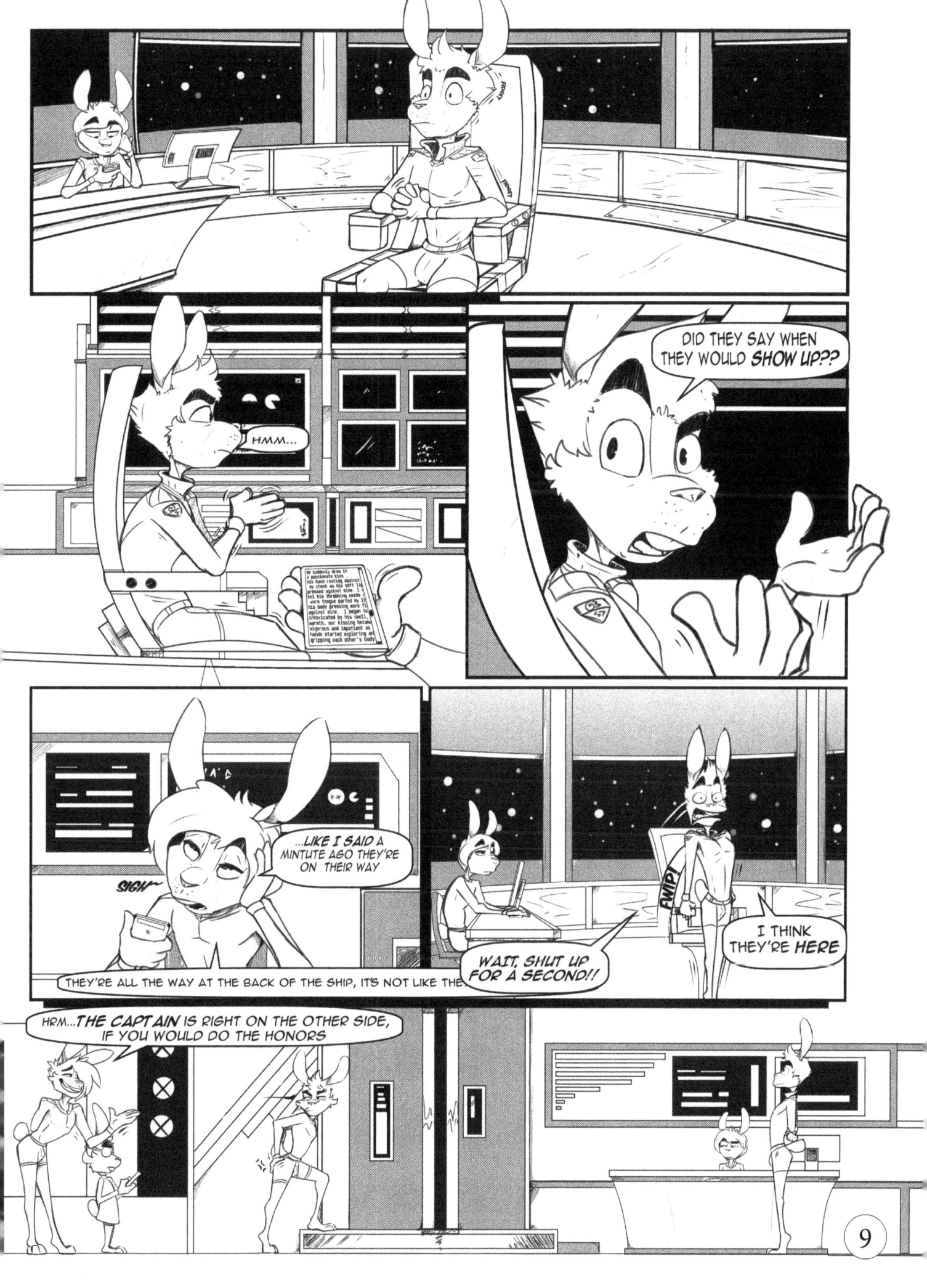

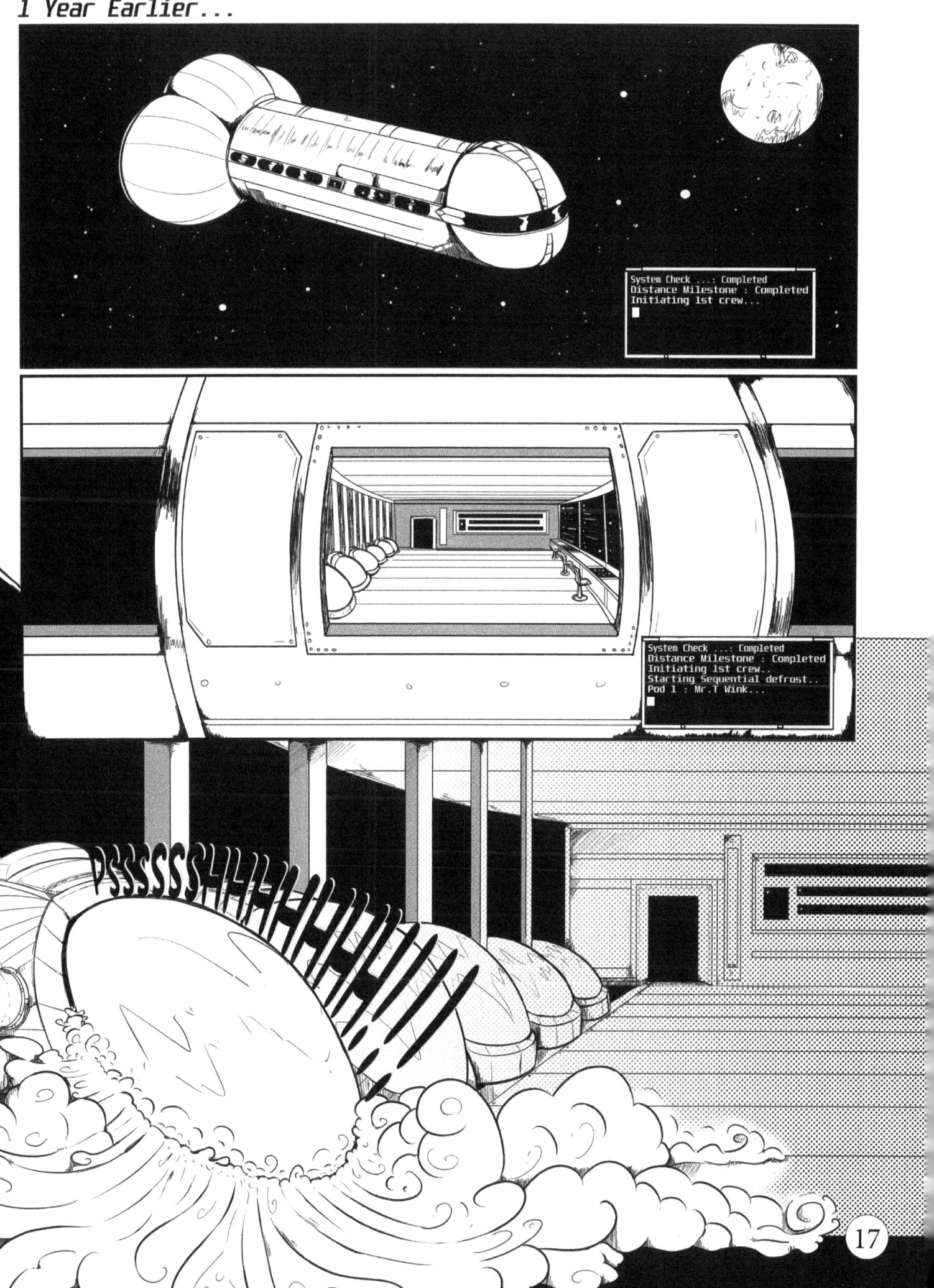

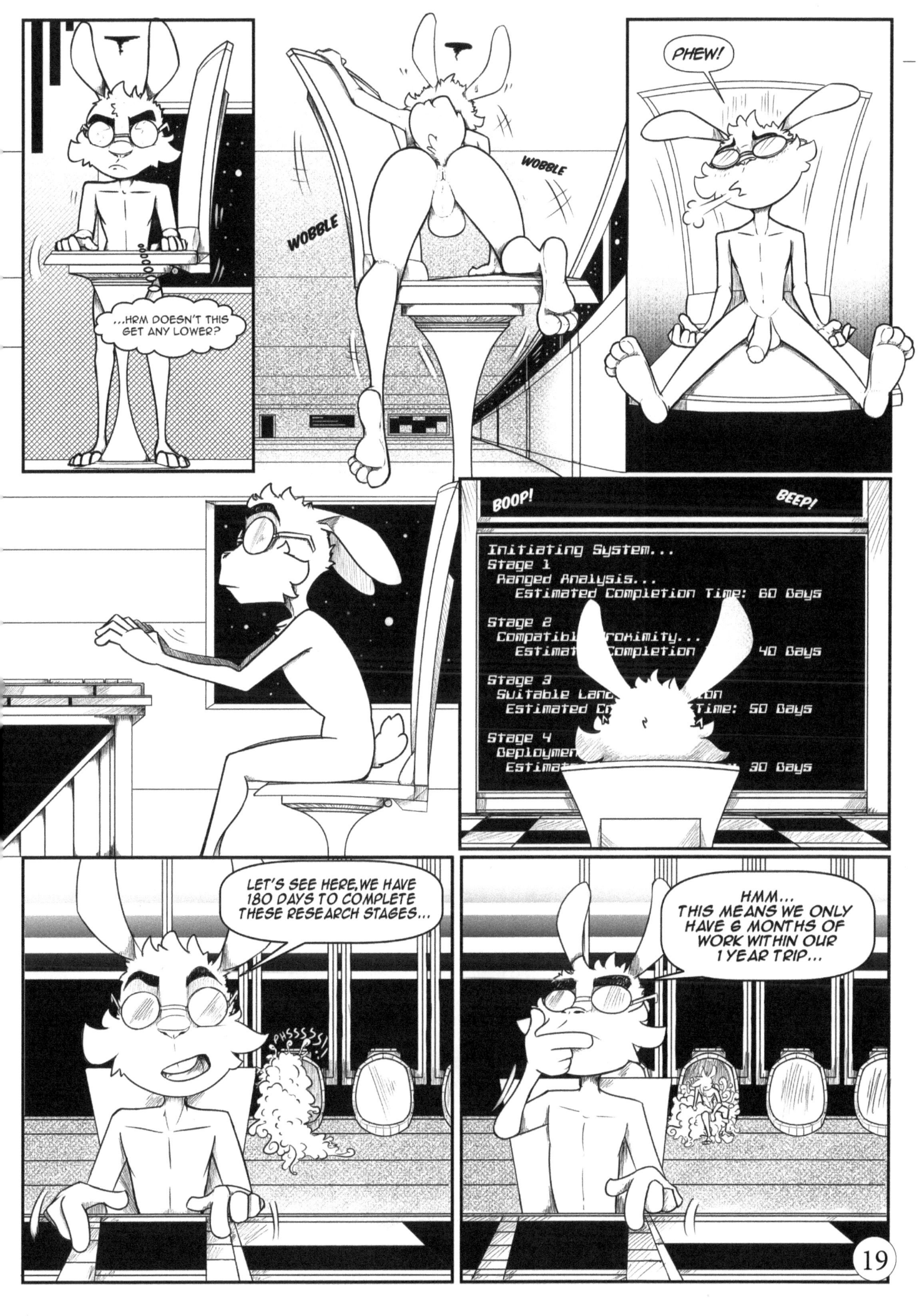

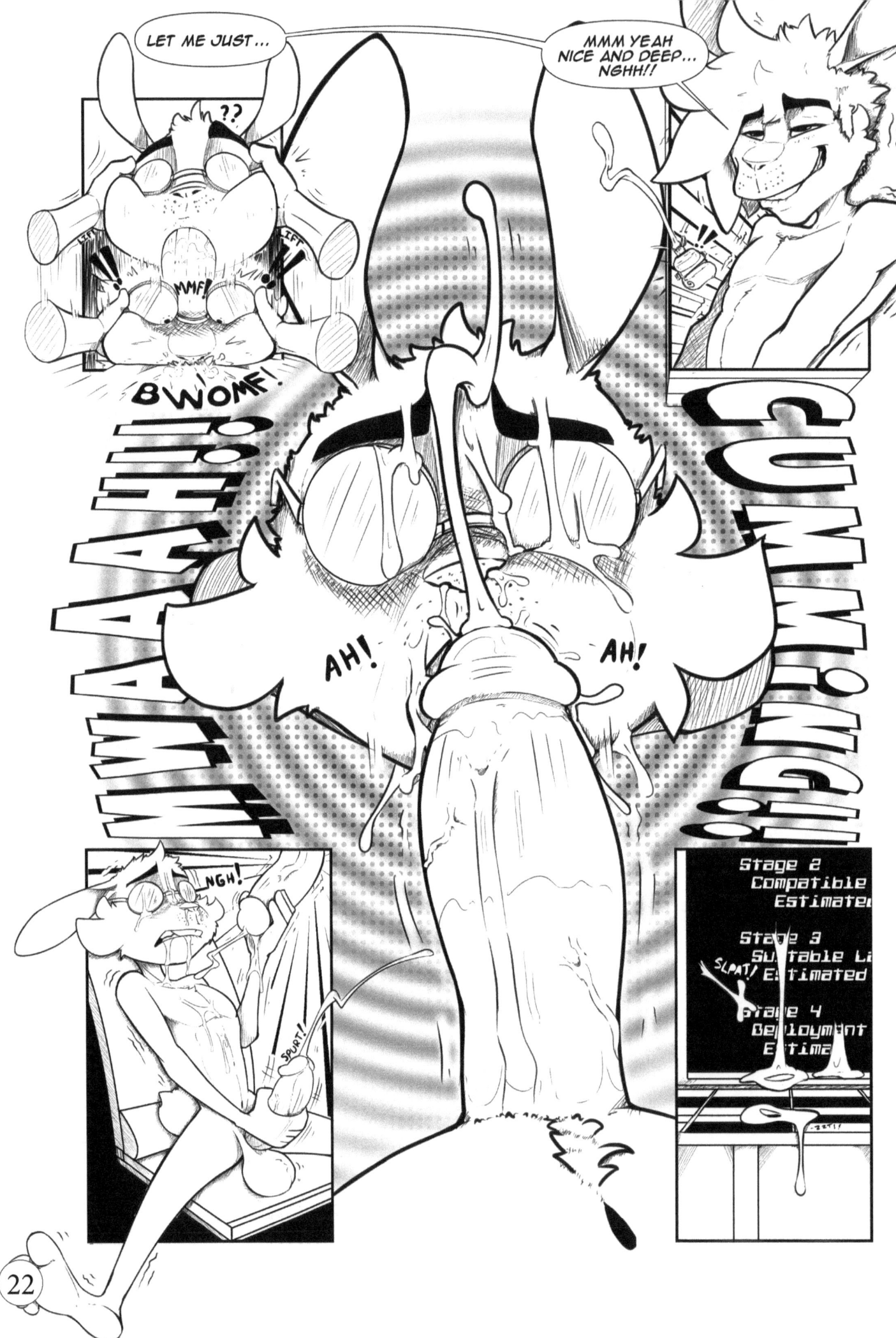

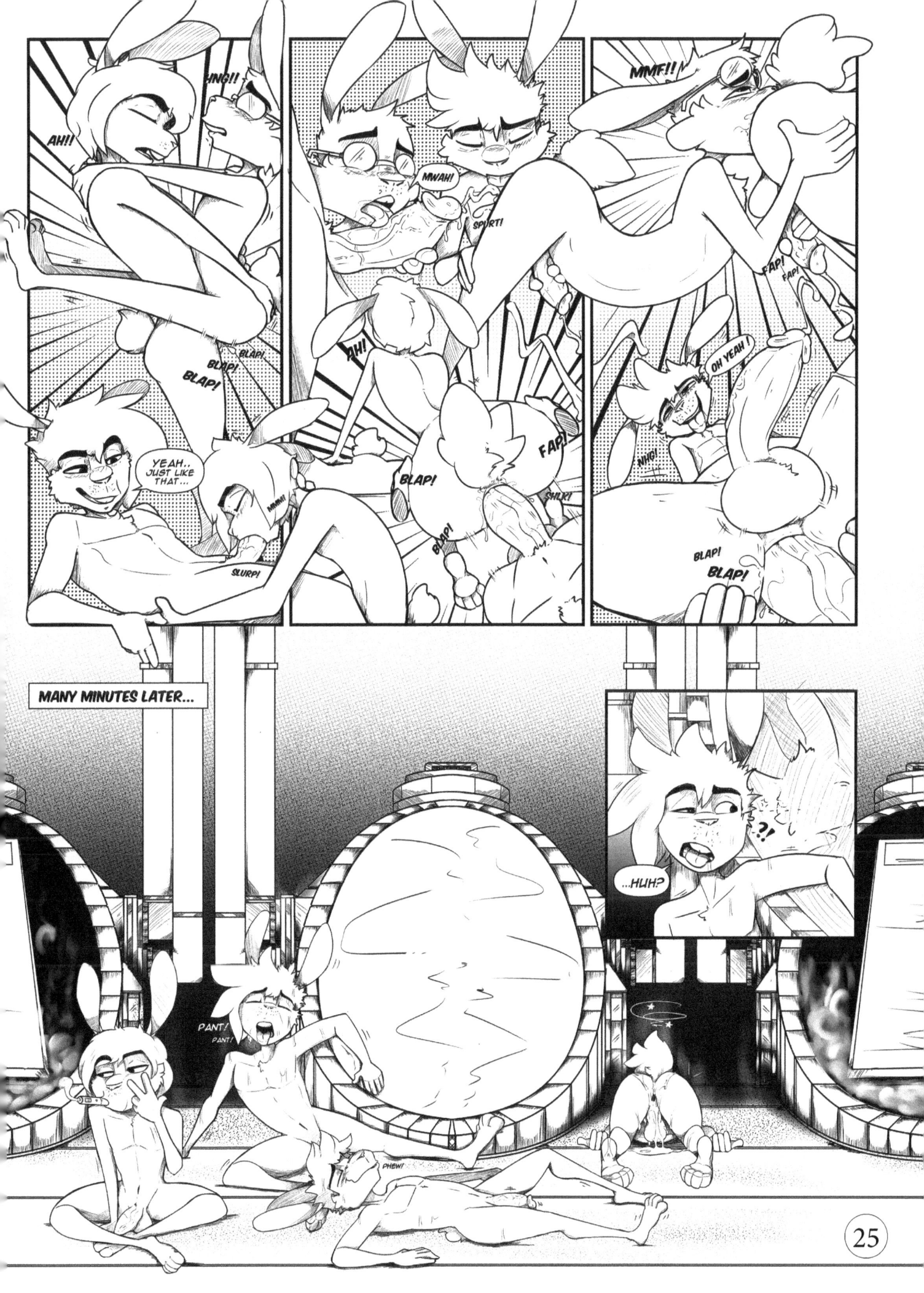

HEY WINK...

WHEN IS THIS GUY WAKING UP?

OH! PLENTY OF TIME TO GET ALL THAT "RESEARCH" DONE... HEH...

MRRNN...UH?

HRMM... OH!...

HE'S THE ENGINEER.... HE'S ONLY SCHEDULED IN ABOUT A YEAR FROM NOW...

AND DONE WITH THE FLASHBACK...

SO THAT'S ROUGHLY HOW THE FIRST DAY WENT

THE SECOND DAY STARTED IN THE SHOWERS...

....

Penile Enlargement Formula
May cause sequential orgasms.
More testing required.

FUN PRODUCTS!

YOUR OWN PERSONAL

VIRTUAL ASSISTANT

- CAN MANAGE YOUR CALENDAR AND TAXES
- CAN BE INTEGRATED INTO ANY VEHICLE FOR DIAGNOSTICS AND MAINTENANCE
- CAN SIMULATE EMOTIONAL SUPPORT
- ROLE PLAYING FUNCTIONS
AND MUCH MORE !

I have no soul!

ONLY 23,000 CREDITS !

GET YOURS TODAY !!

DISCLAIMER: RBT CO IS NOT RESPONSIBLE FOR EMOTIONAL ATTACHMENTS TO YOUR VIRTUAL ASSISTANT. ALL BEHAVIORS ARE PREPROGRAMED AND DO NOT REPRESENT CONSCIOUSNESS. IF YOUR ASSISTANCE IS SHOWING EMPATHY OR ANY RABBIT-LIKE BEHAVIORS PLEASE CONTACT THE MANUFACTURER.

Pure Comfort

No Resistance

COSMO GLIDE INCLUDED !

CERTIFIED

SPEED LIT, I 'LIT SUIT

Galaxy Plumbers

*SATISFACTION GUARANTEED!

* SATISFACTION OF SERVICE DOES NOT NECESSARILY REPRESENT YOUR PLUMBING GETTING REPAIRED

COSMO GLIDE

SPY CAMERA INSERTER!

BUILT IN GPS !

CAN FIT JUST ABOUT ANYWHERE!

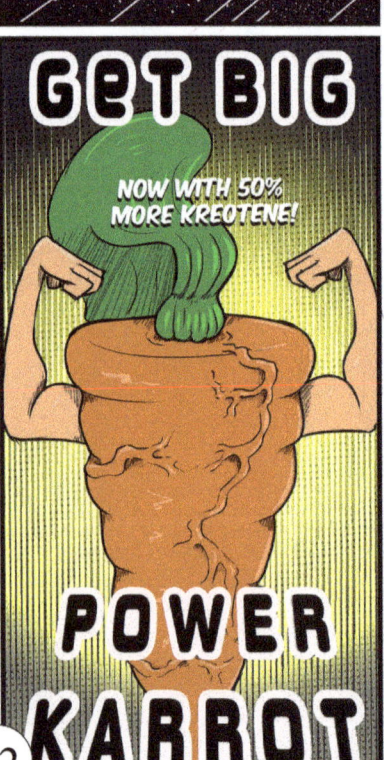

GET BIG

NOW WITH 50% MORE KREOTENE!

POWER KARROT

GEN - BENZ

SWITCH FOR ANY OCCASION!

*NO SIDE EFFECTS !

AND ANYTHING IN-BETWEEN!

HYPNO SPECS!

THEY'LL DO ANYTHING!!

GIVE TO YOUR FRIENDS!

CAUTION: DO NOT STARE IN MIRROR WHEN WEARING HYPNO SPECS

FUN PRODUCTS!

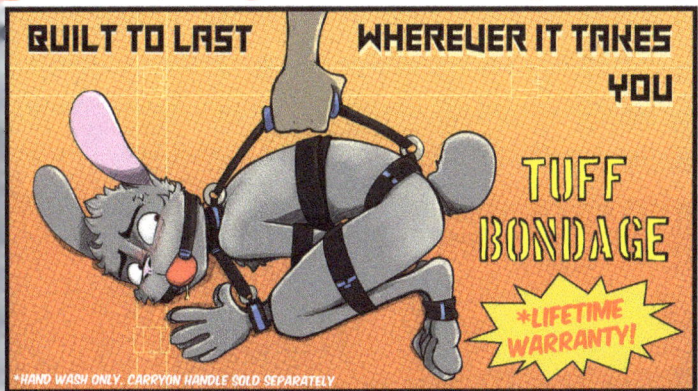

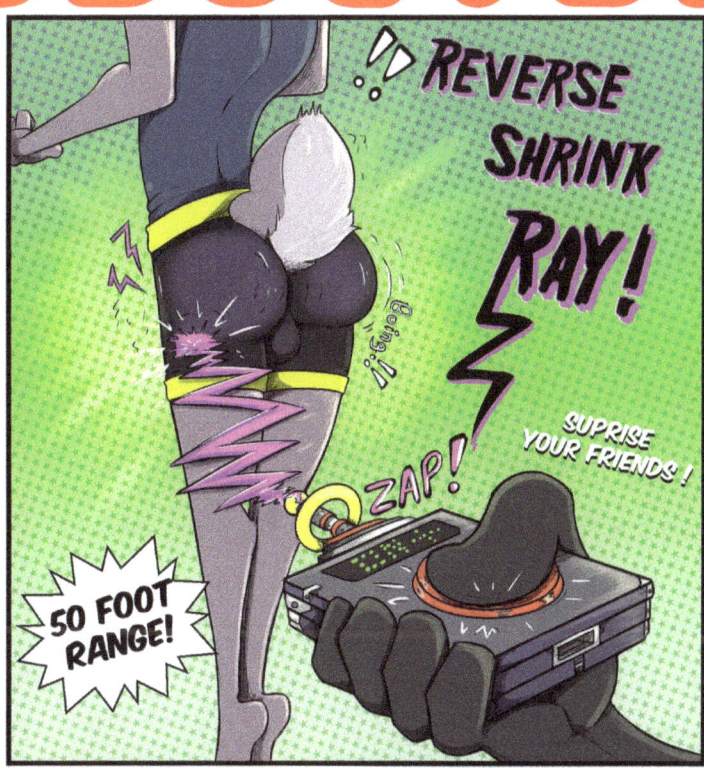

(33)

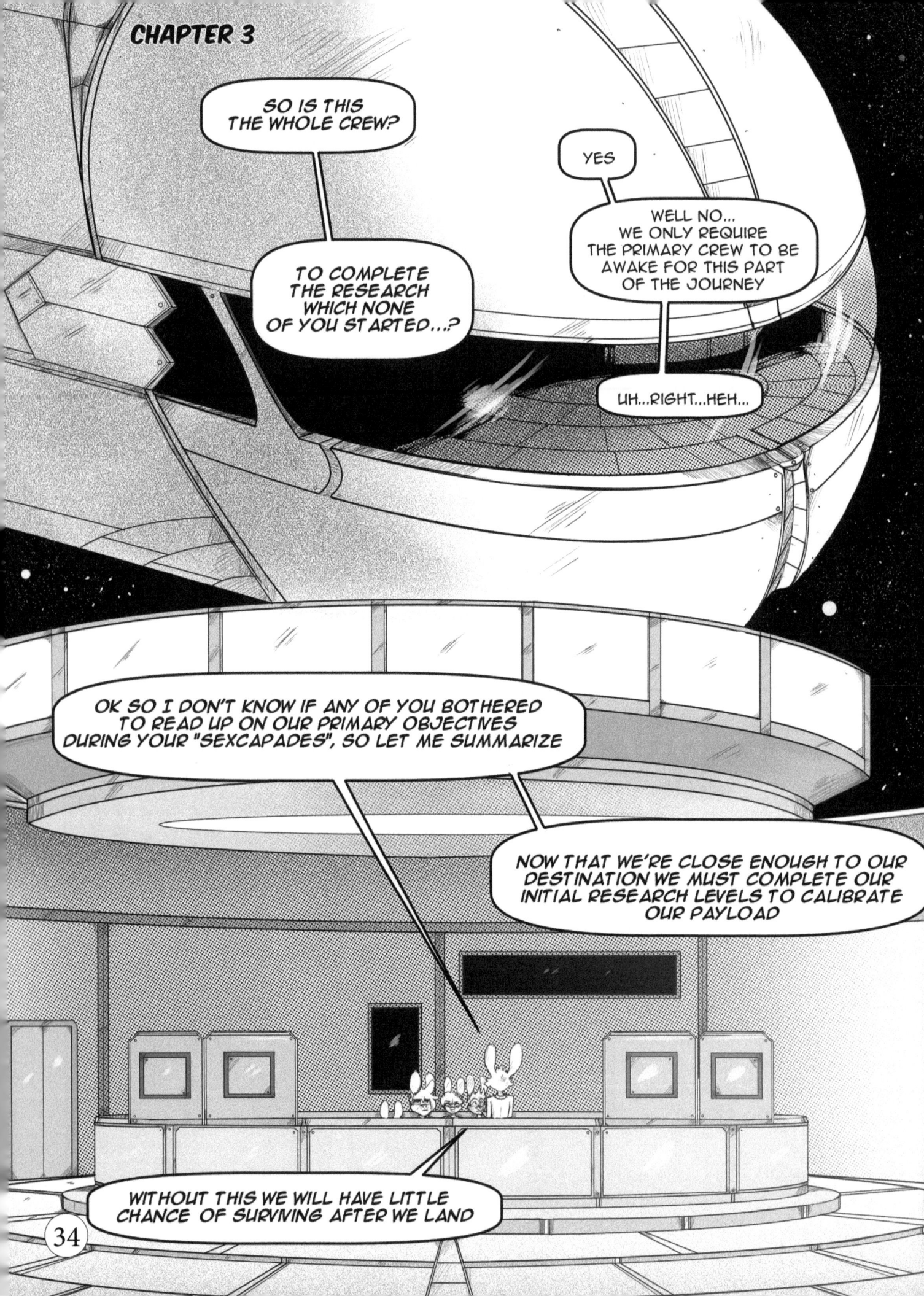

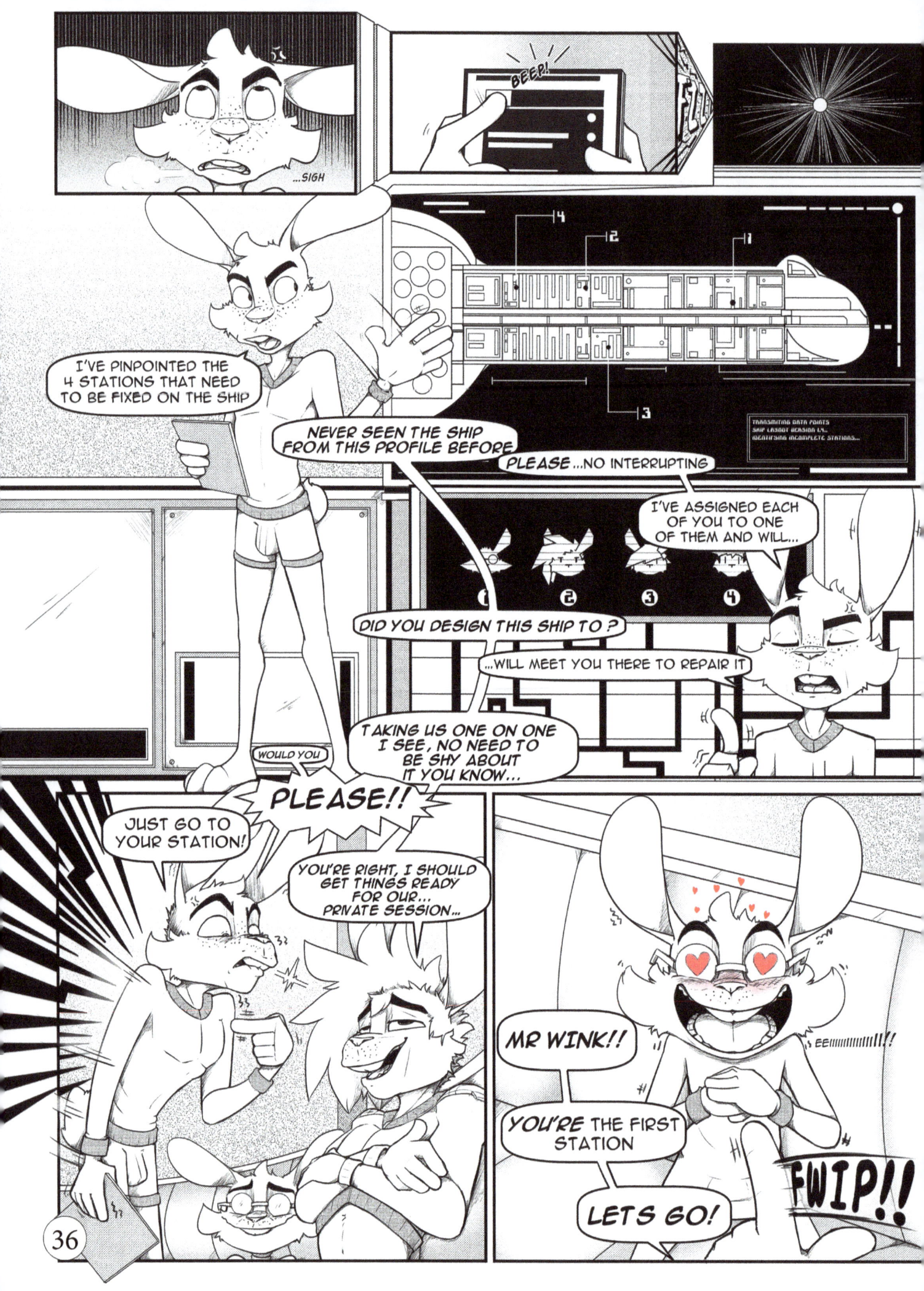

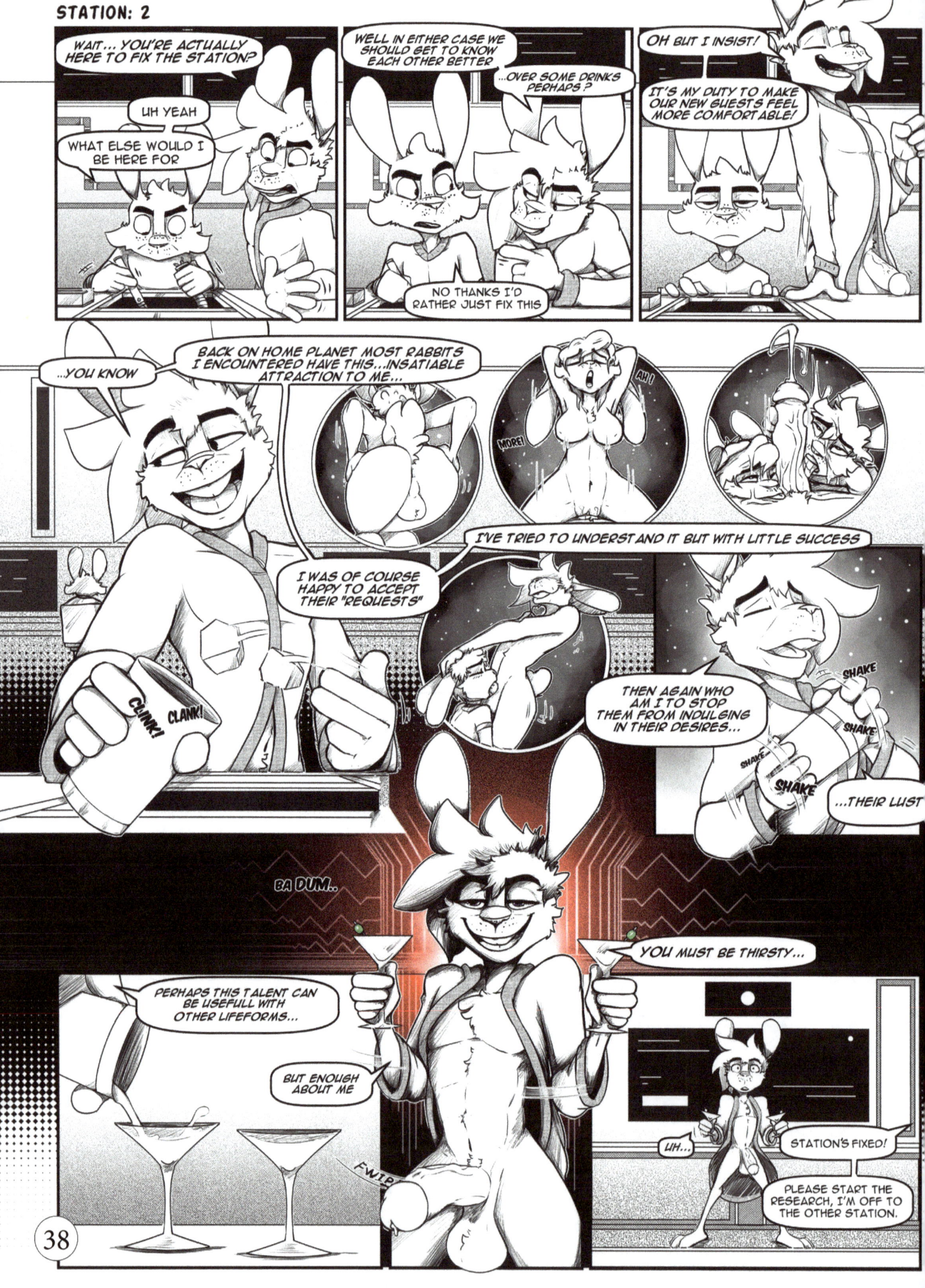

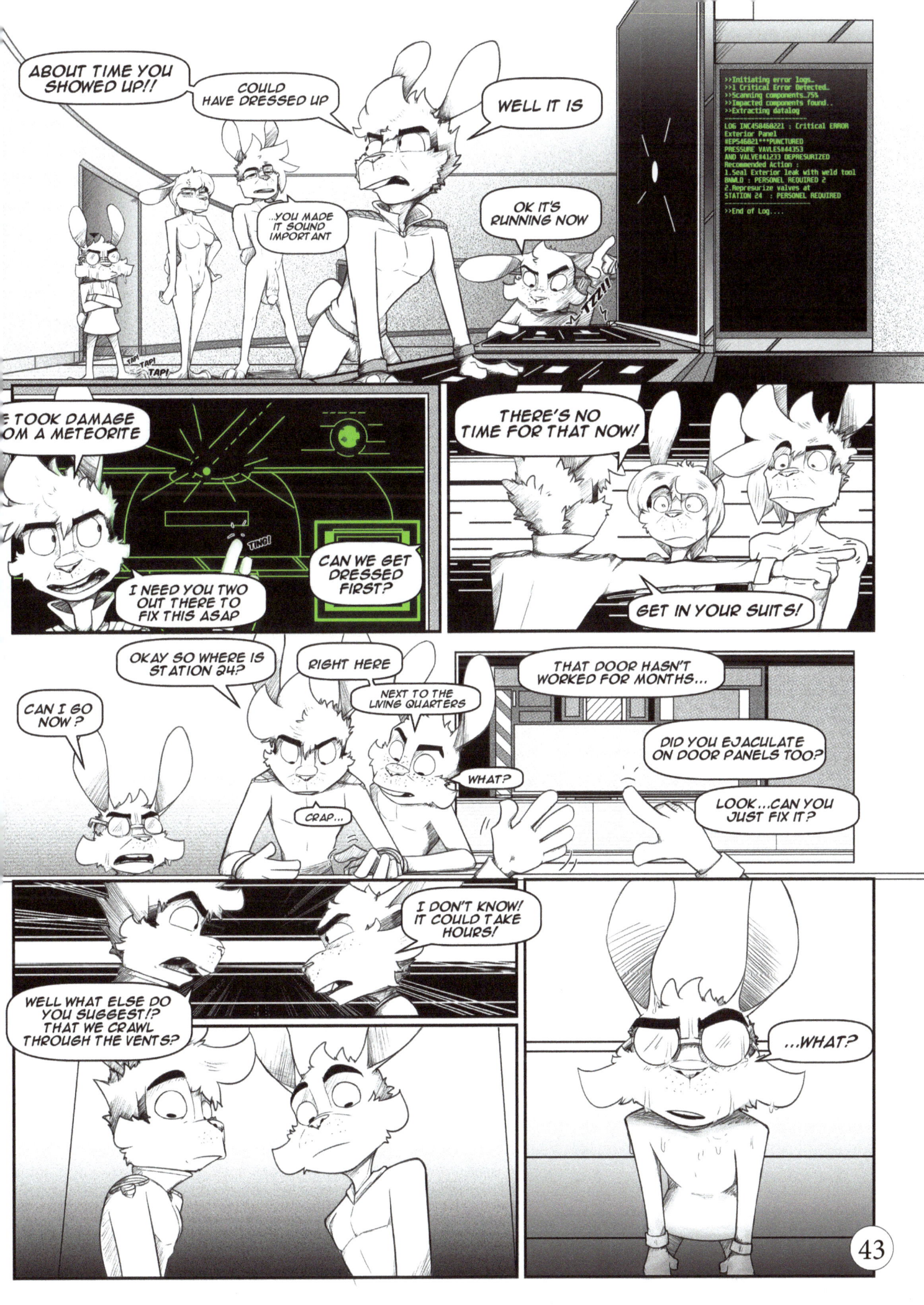

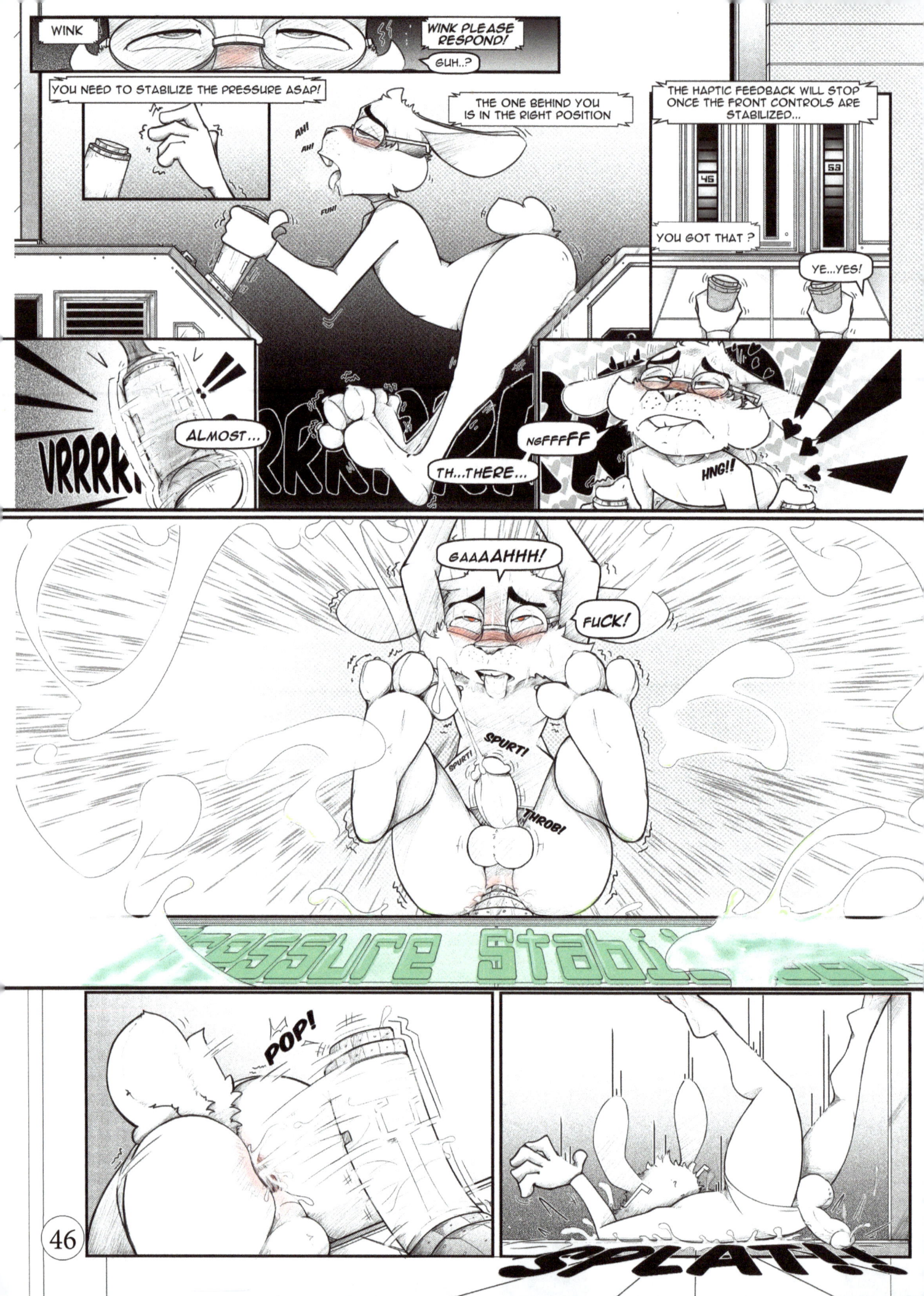

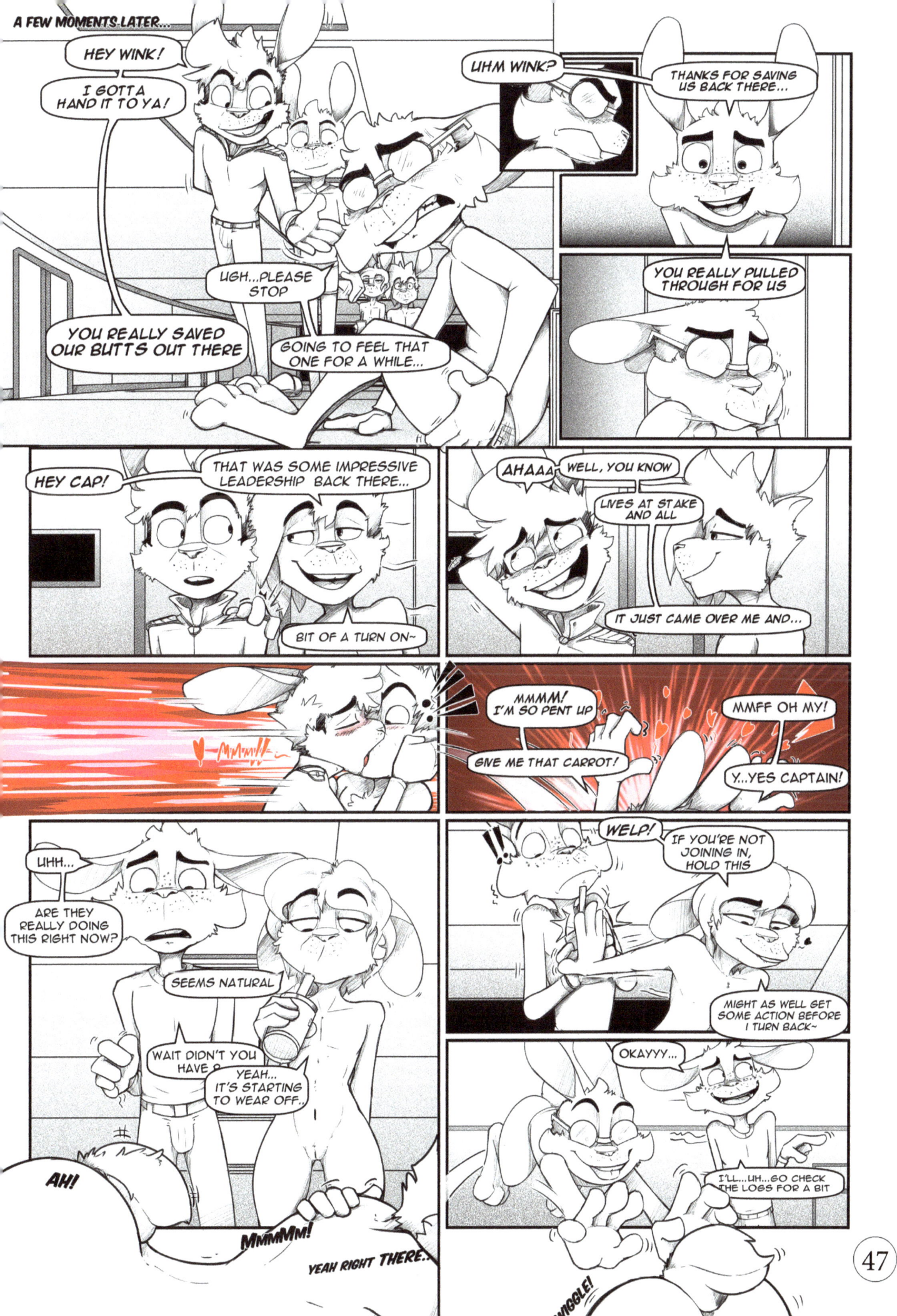

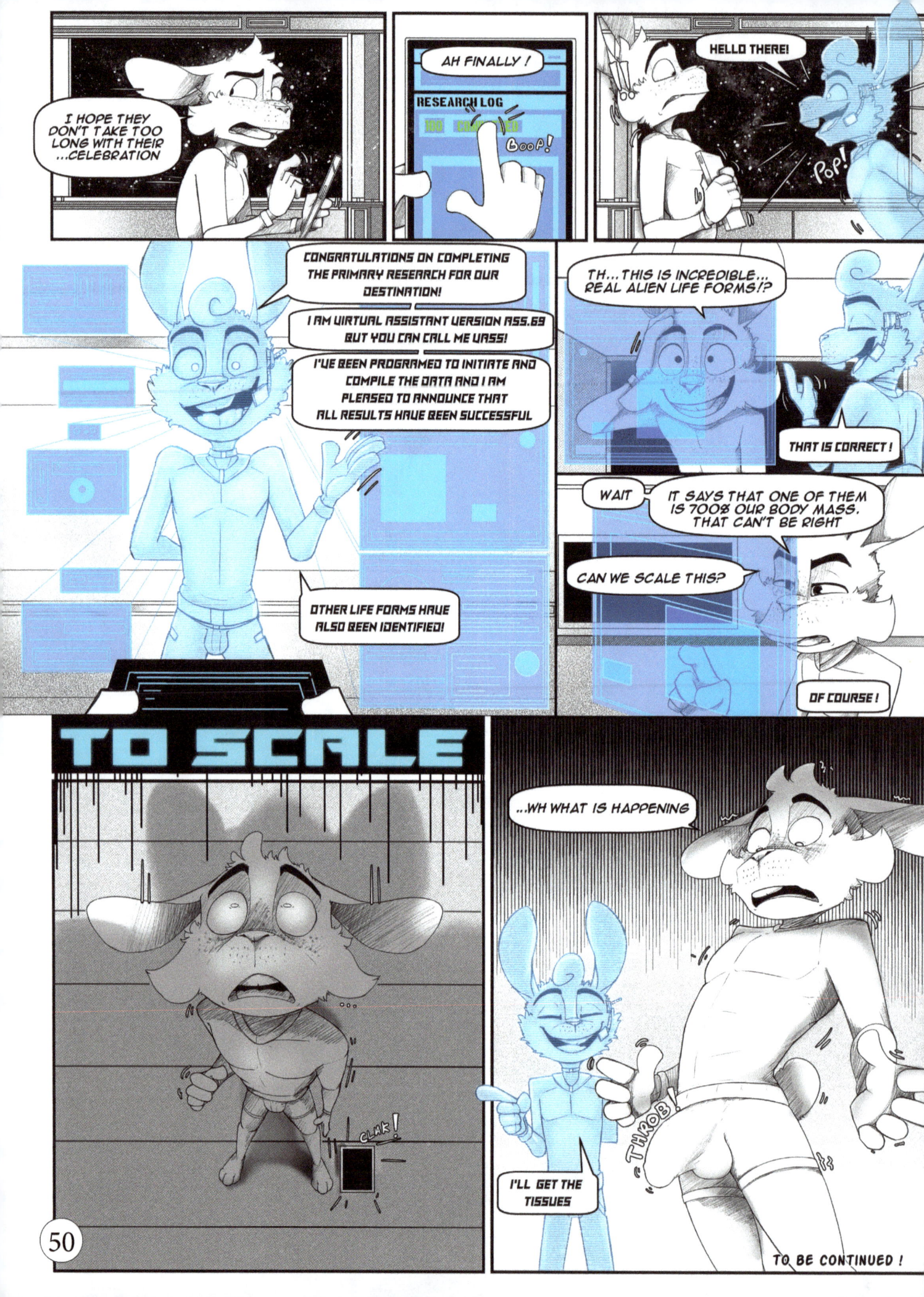

HOPE YOU ENJOYED THIS FIRST VOLUME!
A BIG THANK YOU FOR ALL MY FRIENDS WHO
HAVE ENDURED ME TALKING ABOUT SPACE
RABBITS FOR 2 YEARS STRAIGHT,
AND OF COURSE MY LOVING HUSBAND
WHO I COULD BOUNCE IDEAS OFF CONSTANTLY.

SEE YOU GUYS IN THE NEXT VOLUME!

FIN

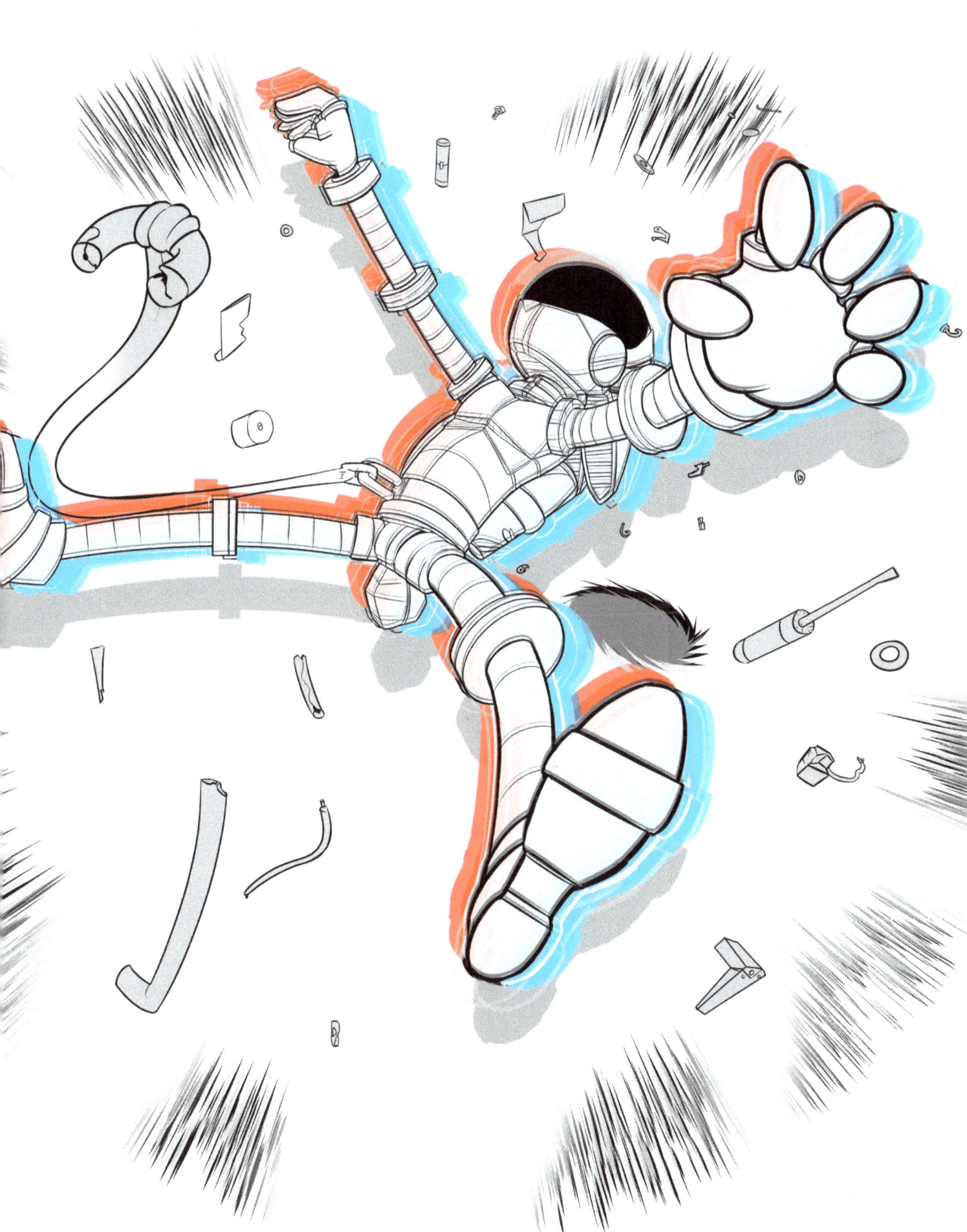